the
SINGING HAT

The
SINGING HAT

TOHBY RIDDLE

FARRAR, STRAUS AND GIROUX / NEW YORK

To Ed and Jasmine Riddle

One fine spring day, Colin Jenkins took the time to sit under a tree. He had not rested for a long while, and sleep soon overcame him.

Colin Jenkins slept deeply and longer than his lunch hour. In fact, when he awoke it was dark, so he made his way home.

All the while, he could not help but notice that people looked at him in ways that he had never been looked at before.

What Colin Jenkins did not know was that while
he slept under the tree in the park, so deeply and
so still, a bird had built a nest on his head.
And there it sat like a rare and peculiar crown.

It was not until Colin Jenkins reached home
that he became aware of this new development.

Colin Jenkins was now faced with quite a conundrum. He could not easily dislodge the perfectly fitted nest from his head, nor did he want to interrupt the bird at such a fragile and important time of life.

Furthermore, his young daughter urged him to leave the poor bird and its egg alone and added that if he sat still long enough she would help feed it.

Colin Jenkins decided—right there and then—that it was not wise to interfere with nature. Having a bird's nest on his head might cause a problem or two, he thought, but he would bear it, so to speak.

From that day on, Colin Jenkins noticed a new world around him. People divided into two groups: those who didn't seem to mind what he had on his head, and those who did.

Colin Jenkins made some new friends…

and lost some old ones.

He wasn't welcome where once he was . . .

meetings at work took on a different character . . .

ordinary occasions did not always remain ordinary.

The bird even made noises as if it were talking.

Life was definitely becoming less usual, Colin Jenkins thought to himself at the end of each day.

One day, Colin Jenkins turned up at work to find he no longer had a job. His boss's reasons for letting him go were not very clear.

Colin Jenkins didn't hear much of it anyway, because an egg was hatching on his head.
"Life goes on," he thought.

As he left the office
building for the last
time, something from
a passing bird spattered
on his shoulder.

"I don't suppose I should take
this personally," reflected
Colin Jenkins, but deep
down he knew he'd had
better days than this.

The arrival of the baby bird had quite an impact on Colin Jenkins's life.

Feeding times in particular were difficult to ignore.

The young bird's first attempts to fly were also difficult to ignore. Nor did they assist Colin Jenkins when trying to get another job.

They didn't seem to assist him in any way at all.
Without work, Colin Jenkins could no longer afford
to keep his home. His landlord, who he'd hoped
might be more understanding of people with birds'
nests on their heads, wasn't.

Of course, it wasn't just landlords who didn't take kindly to people with birds' nests on their heads. Sometimes Colin Jenkins felt alone. And at these times, not even his daughter seemed able to cheer him.

He decided to take action and return
to where this chapter of his life
had begun—to the tree
under which he'd
slept so deeply.

"Maybe I can put this nest in that tree," he hoped.
But when he found the tree he noticed that there
was already a nest in it. He looked at other trees in
the small park . . . It was as if there was no other
home for this nest but the top of his head.

"I suppose it has fallen on me to care for this nest,"
he realized, turning homeward.

"Good heavens, no! It can't be!" exclaimed a man on Colin Jenkins's train. "That bird on your head . . . why, it's possibly the rarest in the world! I thought it had even become extinct!"

The man, who might have been an ornithologist, followed Colin Jenkins out of the train station. "I can't tell you how fortunate it is that these birds are still with us! Not a lot is known about them because sightings are so few. But what we do know . . ."

At that moment the bird took off. The younger bird followed. It seemed to have finally mastered flight, and together the birds soared ever higher into the evening sky.

It looked as if they were gone for good. Colin Jenkins felt a near avalanche of relief. He raised the nest from his head and went to dispose of it.

"Keep the nest," said the man. "The birds have gone, but they may return. That is, if I know my facts about these birds."

Colin Jenkins realized that he was right outside his
home. He turned to say farewell to the man who
might have been an ornithologist, but he was nowhere
to be seen, swallowed up by the rush-hour crowd.

Colin Jenkins went inside and, remembering the man's parting words, placed the nest carefully on a table by the window in his room.

Once off his head, it became a pretty ornament that delighted everyone.

Colin Jenkins never took another job like the one he had, but he always found work. And although he never saw either bird again, from time to time he would find the most beautiful and improbable things . . .

in the nest he had placed on the table by the window in his room.